For Noah x

LITTLE TIGER PRESS
An imprint of Magi Publications
1 The Coda Centre, 189 Munster Road,
London SW6 6AW
www.littletigerpress.com
First published in Great Britain 2001
This edition published 2007
Text and Illustrations © Tim Warnes, 2001
Tim Warnes has asserted his right
to be identified as the author
and illustrator of this work under the
Copyright, Designs and Patents Act, 1988.
All rights reserved
ISBN 978-1-84506-524-9
Printed in China
2 4 6 8 10 9 7 5 3

Can't you sleep, Dotty?

* * *

Tim Warnes

LITTLE TIGER PRESS
London

Dotty couldn't sleep.
It was her first night
in her new home.

She tried sleeping
upside down.

She tried
snuggling up
to Penguin.

She even tried
lying on the
floor.

AWOOOOOOOOOOOoooo°

But still Dotty
couldn't sleep.

Dotty's howling woke up Pip the mouse. "Can't you sleep, Dotty?" he asked. "Perhaps you should try counting the stars like I do."

But Dotty could
only count up to
one. *That* wasn't
enough to send
her to sleep.

What could she do next?

AWOOOOOOOOO

Susie the bird was awake now.

"Can't you sleep, Dotty?" she twittered.

"I always have a little drink before
I go to bed."

chirp!

chirp!

Dotty went to her bowl and
had a little drink.

Slurp!
Slurp!

But then she made
a little puddle.
Well *that*
didn't help!
What *could* Dotty
do to get to sleep?

AWOOOOOOOOO...

Whiskers the rabbit had woken up, too.
"Can't you sleep, Dotty?" he mumbled
sleepily. "I hide away in my burrow
at bedtime. That always works."

Dotty dived under her blanket so
that only her bottom was showing.
But it was all dark under there
with no light at all.

Boing!

Dotty was too scared to go to sleep.

AWOOOOOOOOOOOO

Flump!

Tommy the tortoise
poked his head from
out of his shell.

"Can't you sleep, Dotty?" he sighed.
"I like to sleep where it's bright
and sunny."

Plod
Plod

Dotty liked that idea . . .

. . . and turned on her torch!

"Turn it off, Dotty!"
shouted all her friends.
"*We* can't get to sleep now!"

Poor Dotty was too
tired to try anything else.
Then Tommy had a great idea . . .

He helped Dotty into her bed.
What Dotty needed for the first
night in her new home was . . .

. . . to snuggle up among
all her new friends. Soon
they were all fast asleep.
Night night, Dotty.